D0933901

To Sally, who listened through the fence
CS

In memory of Phylo,
always and everywhere with me
DH

Text copyright © 2022 by Carlie Sorosiak
Illustrations copyright © 2022 by Devon Holzwarth

All rights reserved. No part of this book may be reproduced, transmitted, or stored in an information retrieval system in any form or by any means, graphic, electronic, or mechanical, including photocopying, taping, and recording, without prior written permission from the publisher.

First edition 2022

Library of Congress Catalog Card Number pending
ISBN 978-1-5362-1497-0

21 22 23 24 25 26 APS 10 9 8 7 6 5 4 3 2 1

Printed in Humen, Dongguan, China

This book was typeset in Horley Old Style.
The illustrations were done in mixed media.

Walker Books US
an imprint of
Candlewick Press
99 Dover Street
Somerville, Massachusetts 02144

www.walkerbooksus.com

orosiak, Carlie,
verywhere with you /
022.
3305250245002
a   08/03/22

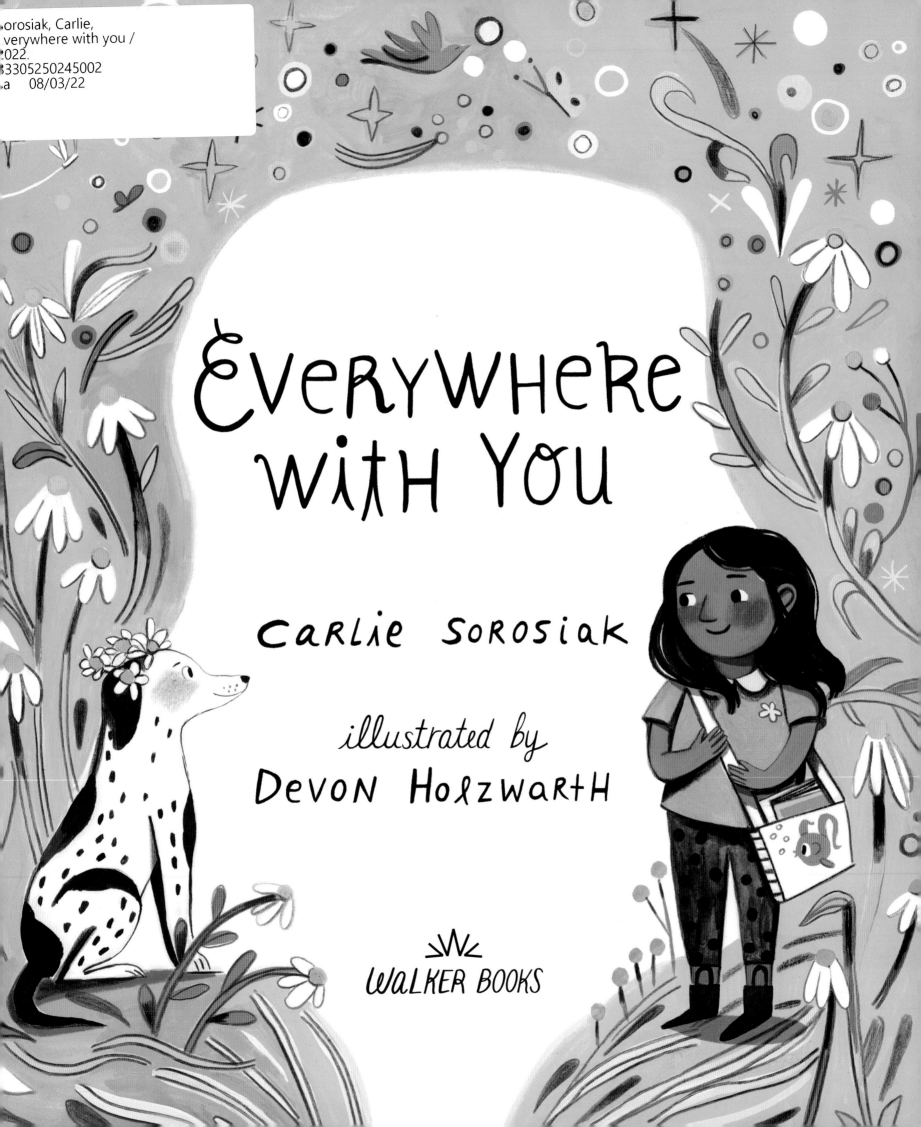

Everywhere with You

Carlie Sorosiak

illustrated by
Devon Holzwarth

WALKER BOOKS

Here are two houses.
And that's a fence between them.

On one side is a dog.
Every night he howls under the star-speckled sky,
or digs large holes by the overgrown hedges.
Sometimes he glances back at his tail, watching it move—
just so he feels less alone.

His ears always perk at night noises:
bush critters jumping, elm branches
swaying,
and now—
right now—
f o o t s t e p s,
soft through the grass
on the other side of the fence.

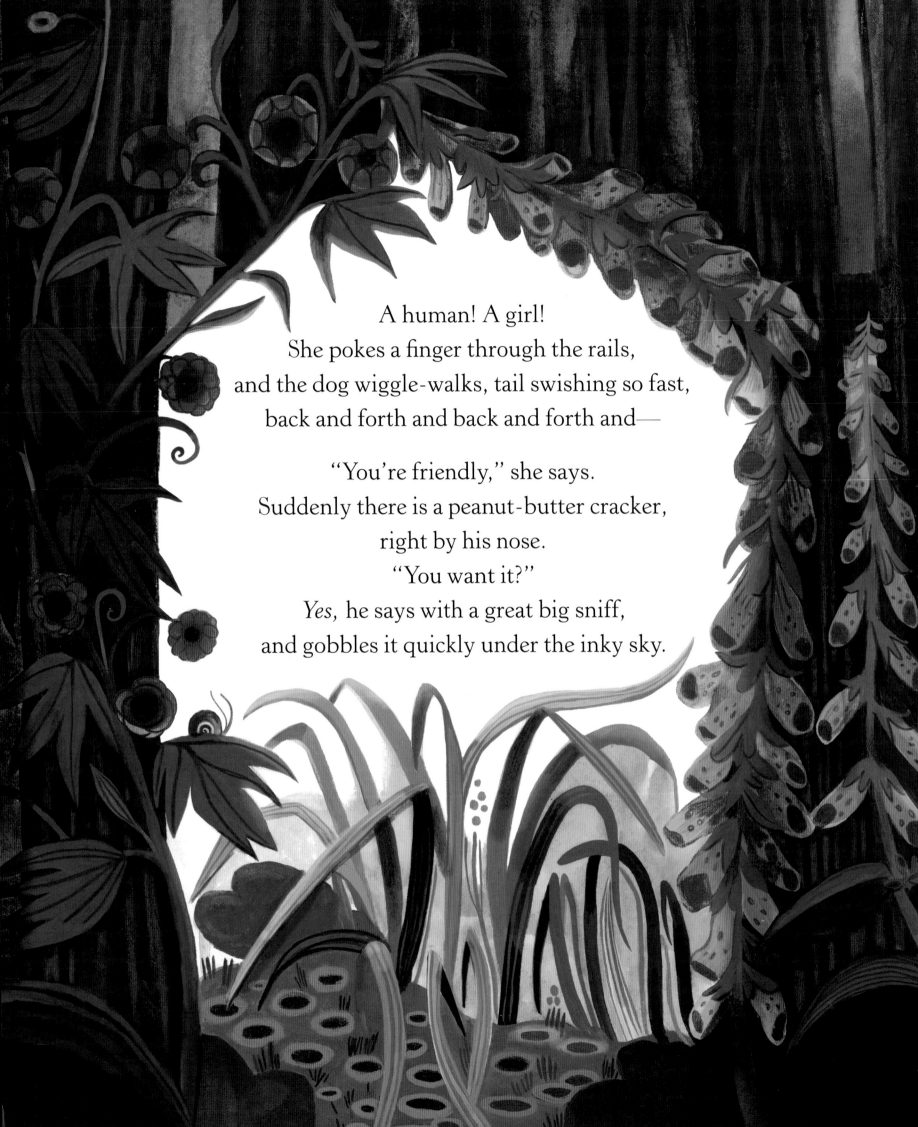

A human! A girl!
She pokes a finger through the rails,
and the dog wiggle-walks, tail swishing so fast,
back and forth and back and forth and—

"You're friendly," she says.
Suddenly there is a peanut-butter cracker,
right by his nose.
"You want it?"
Yes, he says with a great big sniff,
and gobbles it quickly under the inky sky.

She comes back the next night,
too—when the clouds grow dark,
when the porch lights flicker—
books balanced in her arms.

"I hope you don't mind,"
she says.

"I've noticed that no one ever plays
with you—and I like reading aloud.
These are my favorites."

He doesn't mind at all. Her voice curls
like a ribbon in the dark.

The first story is about a deep-sea kingdom—
shimmering mermaids, emerald fins.
In his mind, he's underwater.
He's there.

That night he has
magnificent dreams.

Soon, every time the sun sets, the girl appears at the fence,
sharing cheddar snacks with him,
reading books with him.

"Have you ever wanted," she asks, "to be someone else?"

So they become pirates
and dragon riders
and magicians with silver wands.

She keeps reading.
In fall,
in winter,
in spring . . .

In summer, she brings out cool pops
and reads stories as the fireflies
glint around them.

That's the best part.

The worst part is goodbye.

"Tomorrow?"

Tomorrow.

All day, he waits for night noises.
For the screen door opening.
For her footsteps in the summer grass.

Then one night, he sees something
through bright windows next door:
the girl and her parents, circled around a table,
playing a game.

The sound of laughter trickles into the yard.

He's never been inside a human house.
He can feel it all—
how the girl and her family are together,
how they love one another.
And he wants this, to be with them,
more than all the stars in the sky.

Digging at the warm earth—
but the ground is too hard.

Leaping through the night air—
but the fence is too high.

So he has to wait.
He has no choice but to wait
and howl
as loud
as he can.

The girl bursts from her house
and runs to the fence.

"It's OK," she says, pressing her nose to his. "It's OK. I'm here."

Nightjars croon.
Fireflies flit.
"Did you know," the girl whispers,
"that this is my favorite time of day? Being here with you?"
And he tells her with soft eyes,
Mine! It is mine, too.

That evening, the girl spins a story of her own—
the two of them,
sailing to a forgotten island,
breaking an ancient curse,
tearing down an enchanted wall.

It's the best story yet.

Nights later, the sky erupts:
thunder and lightning and sideways rain.
Whoosh! Whoosh!

Just like that, a hole.

He picks his way through,
f o o t s t e p s
careful, like the girl's.

Barking at the back door:
It's me! It's me!

Fingers in his fur:
"It's you! It's you!"

In a new room, a towel ruffles his coat.

"I just spoke with the neighbors,"
her mom says.
"They've seen you reading together,
and have been wondering for a while:
Would we like to keep him?"

"Where should we travel tonight?"
the girl asks, after he's clean and dry
and home.
"A secret garden?
The circus?
A new world?"

Anywhere, he says.
And everywhere, with you.